Game of Hearts

ENCHANTED WISHES COLLECTION

VIOLA TEMPEST

VIOLA TEMPEST PUBLISHING

Copyright

GAME OF HEARTS

Enchanted Wishes Collection

© Copyright 2023 Viola Tempest

Cover Design by Fay Lane Cover Design

Contents

Game *of* HEARTS

ENCHANTED WISHES COLLECTION

VIOLA TEMPEST

Roman rushed through the toy aisle at the department store, searching doll after doll. It was the fourth store he had tried that day, on top of the three he'd already stopped at the day before. But still, as his eyes skimmed for that bright pink and baby blue package — for the Barbie that Sadie had so eagerly begged for — he came up empty.

He stopped as an empty row sat nestled between two other Barbies. He leaned down to look closer at the price tag.

Barbie: Queen of the Mermaids. $30.00.

Roman clenched his thick fingers into a tight fist. They were gone here, too. How?! Why? Why was this stupid mermaid Barbie the chosen one for this year's little girls? And why had his sweet little niece been among the thousands of others who wanted this plastic doll?

Roman huffed as he stomped back out of the store and made his way through the brisk February chill to his car. People all around him were joyous and cuddling as the holiday of love lingered only a week away. Girls giggled into their friends' shoulders over boys' pictures on their phones. Women had a mix of stress lines and frustrated frowns on their faces as they checked their phones every few minutes. Men rushed in and out of the store, raiding the candy aisle, the flower displays at the front, and yanking giant stuffed animals out of cardboard bins near the cash registers.

All of these people prepared for Valentine's Day, while Roman slammed his car door shut and sped in the direction of downtown, looking for a plastic doll for his niece's birthday. Which just so happened to be in two hours. And his front seat was still empty of bags. He had only one envelope, wrapped around a blue and purple card with a mermaid on the front. She smiled tauntingly at him as if she knew his stress. She knew he had failed to find the only gift he promised Sadie this year. She knew how terrible of an uncle he was. She knew everything of his shortcomings.

He flipped the card over and sped up.

He was going to be late to the party if he didn't hurry. Maybe if he could make one more stop at the department store in Evansville. It was only another twenty-five minutes away and then twenty-five back, plus fifteen more to get to his sister's. As long as there weren't any accidents on the highway and rush hour traffic wasn't bad, he'd be just in time.

He gripped the wheel tighter as the urbanized part of town thinned out, and the close houses and small shops along downtown Main Street started to form. Sweat beaded on his brow as he saw red and blue lights dance further down the road. People's brake lights flared in front of him as they all slowed to a stop.

"No, *no!* Come on!" Roman yelled. He leaned back and forth, trying to get a better look at the damage, but all he could see was the butt end of a busted up semi-truck alongside a police cruiser. "Okay, okay. It's fine. I'll just turn around and go up Route 45 instea—"

Roman tried backing up enough to turn around, but the person behind him was too close, and the person on their tail was even closer. He wasn't going anywhere. He slammed a fist onto the steering wheel, and with his blasted horn, a shrill chorus of horns mimicked him. Roman laid his head against the cold steering wheel. Not today. He couldn't do this today. He didn't have time!

He glanced at the clock on his dash — *5:35pm*. An hour and a half. Wonderful. Just wonderful. He'd never make it to Evansville and back now. He might not even make it out of downtown in time, with the rate things were going — forget the Barbie.

Roman peered out of his window, trying to get a better view. That's when he noticed the small shop nestled in the back of the busy street among two huge weeping willow trees. He squinted at the unlit sign in the dim light of the evening sun and just barely made out "Aunt May's Antique Shop" swirled in loopy cursive. Roman had been downtown hundreds of times before. He lived only ten minutes away on the other end of their small town. But this shop... he had never seen it before. Never even heard its name.

He didn't know what it was. Maybe the stress of the last two days. Maybe his dire need to get *something* for Sadie. Maybe because of the hopeless situation he found himself sitting in. Whatever it was, he found himself turning his wheel in the direction of the shop and parking his truck out front.

A low, dim light burned from the inside, and he took this as his invitation to enter. The door creaked violently as he entered and squealed as he pushed it shut behind him. As he glanced around, he realized that the "antique" part of the shop's name was right. Everything was covered in a layer of dust. The furniture was stained and worn with the stories of people's past. The wooden table at the front of the shop had cracks lining its surface and rings from old cups. Rusted tools, dated patterned fabric, crinkling book spines, and colorful ceramic models lined shelf after shelf as he walked further into the room.

"Hello?" Roman called out. But only silence answered him.

He rounded a corner, entering into another room, and then another, until he found the back of the shop. He heard a cough, brittle and raspy like that of an old smoker. He made his way toward the sound in the next room, but it, too, was empty. He sighed as he went to retrace his steps, but his eyes caught onto something in the back corner of the last room. He peered closer into the dim light and found an old shoebox, torn at the corners and faded with age, lying on top of a wooden table. It was open, and its contents were covered with a thin layer of tissue paper.

Roman didn't know why he felt compelled to that box. Why he felt the need to explore its contents. Why he was drawn so closely to this exact place at this exact time. But in that moment, he needed to know what was inside. He peeled back the crinkling layer of paper and unveiled —

A tiny teacup with a doll in it.

Her porcelain white face glowed in the last rays of sunlight seeping in through the torn blinds over the window. Her blonde hair glimmered and curled around her gentle jaw. Her painted lips curled into a coy smile that didn't quite reach her large blue eyes. The rest of her body was petite, dressed in a faded blue dress with white lace details. She had white gloves to match, and a tiny handbag perched under one elbow.

Roman stared down at this doll and found that he couldn't take his eyes away. That smile — those eyes — they knew something about him. It felt like they could see right through him.

"Ahem." A throat crackled behind him, nearly making him jump out of his skin.

Roman eyed the wrinkled and hunched woman in the doorway, just as she, too, peered at him.

"Can I help you, young man?" She croaked, that

thick smoker's drawl reminding him of the cough he'd heard before.

"Yes, uh. I'm sorry to intrude. I just made my way in and started admiring all your... antiques." Roman coughed nervously as he brushed his dusty hands on the bottom of his shirt.

The woman took a step closer and glanced behind him. Her lips curled into an almost toothless smile.

"Found the doll, eh?"

"What? Oh, uh, yes." Roman glanced over his shoulder at the porcelain beauty.

"A gift for your girl I suppose? Interesting choice for Valentine's though."

"No! No, um, I'm not... no."

The woman's brow raised in question. "You're single then."

Roman shuffled his feet. Why were they having this conversation? Didn't he need to be somewhere?

Sadie!

"Actually, I was looking for a gift for my niece. It's her birthday today, and I'm on my way to her party. She loves dolls, and I thought this might do. Don't you think? She's beautiful."

The woman nodded slowly. "She is. She is... one of a kind, that one. Her beauty is unparalleled, but don't let that trick you. She toys with every man"

Roman watched the woman as it was his turn to raise an eyebrow. What did she mean?

"Anyway, I'm sure you'll be fine. It *is* a gift, after all. Now, are you going to pay with cash or card?" The woman waved as she made her way through to the next room and back toward the front of the shop.

Roman eyed the doll one more time, the woman's strange words ringing in his head. His phone beeped, and he checked the time. *6:15pm*. Shit! How had it gotten so late? He grabbed the box and closed it tight before rushing out of the shop and racing to his sister's.

SADIE LOVED THE DOLL. It wasn't Barbie — Queen of the Mermaids — as promised, but it was unique and beautiful, and Sadie couldn't stop smiling at her new toy. As soon as she unboxed the porcelain girl, she brushed back her hair, straightened her clothes, and wiped down her fair face with a wet cloth to remove all the dust.

She named the doll Vivien. Sadie and Vivien hadn't separated once since Roman's arrival.

After a long evening of dinner — Sadie's favorite, spaghetti and meatballs — present opening, cake cutting, board game playing, and joking around, everyone outside the family eventually left. Now, it was only Roman, his younger sister, Olivia, and Sadie left. The three of them sat in the living room, Roman and Olivia on the sofa, sparingly watching some Hallmark romance movie on TV, while Sadie played with Vivien the doll on the carpet.

"Oh, John. It's always been you, hasn't it? You were my secret admirer all along."

John took Kate's hands in his own. "I was too afraid to reveal myself earlier. But now... I'm more afraid of not telling you and losing that chance forever. Kate — I want to spend the rest of my life with you."

Kate gasped.

The two characters on the screen then ogled at each other as snow fell around them in a light flurry. Olivia snorted as Roman feigned swooning at the confession.

"Marry me, Kate. And I will love you every day for the rest of my life."

"Yes!" Kate jumped with joy, and John scooped her up into a hug. The two kissed in the final minute of the movie, and the screen faded to black as the credits followed.

Olivia groaned. "I always hate these movies. They're so unrealistic."

"I think that's the point." Roman chuckled. "They

always end with a happy ending. Everyone wants a happy ending."

"I guess."

"You don't?" He raised a brow at his sister.

Olivia leaned back onto the couch and sighed. "Of course, I do. It's just... not as satisfying knowing that those people started and will continue a relationship with almost no foundation built. They didn't go through hardship together or work to make a life together. They just found each other, fell in love at first sight, and then poof! Happy ever after. Real relationships take time, energy, and effort from both people."

"Yeah, you're right, I guess."

Olivia nudged him. "How's the dating front been for you lately? Any dates set for Valentine's Day?"

Roman laughed. "No luck so far. I can't even dream of falling in love and living a perfect little life with my Hallmark movie soulmate because I can't seem to meet anyone. Good or bad."

"It takes time. It'll happen when it happens. You can't rush love."

"Very soothing advice. Thank you."

Olivia chuckled as she pushed herself up from the couch. "Hey, chin up. Ms. Right will come along soon enough. You just have to be patient."

Roman nodded quietly, and Olivia seemed to take that as her cue to move on.

"Sadie, come on. Bed time."

Sadie groaned and asked for five more minutes, but Olivia remained stubborn. She told her to leave Vivien downstairs so she didn't get damaged in Sadie's "travesty of a room," as Olivia so lovingly referred to it. Roman gave Sadie a tight squeeze as the girl hugged him goodnight. She thanked him one more time for her present and ran up the stairs, all memory of her protest to stay awake and play suddenly gone.

Olivia told him she'd be back down in a bit, and she followed Sadie up the stairs. Roman sat silently in the living room as the next Hallmark movie started playing. He grabbed the remote and tried switching the channel, but it wouldn't cooperate. He sighed as he pressed the button again and again, but the TV didn't respond. Roman grunted as he pushed himself up and made his way to the TV. He felt for a button along its side, something that could change the blasted channel, but it was smooth.

"Can't stand seeing what you don't have?" A high-pitched voice squeaked from behind him.

Roman whipped around, but the room was empty. He swore he had just heard a voice, but no one was here. He turned to the TV again.

"I agree with you; those relationships are all abhorrently fake."

Roman turned as the voice, sweet like honey, continued on.

"You don't need something like that. You need something real. Something that will last." Roman looked down at the doll, who was now standing straight up on the carpet. She had a hip bumped to one side and an elbow perched there. She grinned at Roman's wide eyes. "What kind of woman are you into exactly, Roman?"

Roman nearly knocked the TV over when he scurried away from the animated doll. He crashed onto the carpet and crawled backwards as she stepped, one poised foot in front of the other. Her pink lips curled into a crooked smile as she stepped toward him.

"What? What are you?" he stuttered.

She laughed. "I'm Vivien. The doll you picked up from the antique shop. You know this."

"Yeah. But... but how?"

Vivien rolled her eyes. "It doesn't matter how. What matters is *why*, Roman. And *why* I'm here today with you, is because you chose me at the shop. You see, I'm chosen only when I'm needed. So, you, dear Roman, must have needed my services."

"Your... services?"

"Yes. And so close to Valentine's Day, too. How fitting." At Roman's silent stare, Vivien sighed. "I'm a matchmaker, silly. Men choose me, they tell me the traits they find desirable in a woman, and I give them an array of options to choose from. Sounds exciting, doesn't it?"

Roman hesitated at the light dancing in Vivien's glassy eyes. Something... something wasn't quite right. But Vivien's warm smile put him at ease.

"Now tell me, Roman, what do you look for in a woman?"

"Um, well, I like women who are sweet, warm, and cute. Preferably someone who likes to read, like me. She could be an academic or not, doesn't really matter."

"What would your dream woman's career be?"

Roman scratched his chin. "Maybe a teacher or a librarian. Perhaps a nurse or a vet. Something where she could help and work with others."

Vivien nodded slowly like she was weighing his answer. "And her appearance?"

Roman smiled sheepishly. "I like blondes. Brunettes are alright, and red heads are eye-catching, too. But I suppose I prefer blondes the most. Blue or green eyes, fair skin, freckles, petite shape, just fit enough to be healthy without being overly muscular."

"And her social status... how does she interact with others?"

"What do you mean?"

"Is your dream woman very sociable, more of an

extrovert? Or is she more quiet and subtle and intro-verted? What does her social life look like, and what does she like to do in her spare time?"

"Well, I think my ideal woman would be more extroverted than me, which wouldn't be too difficult," he chuckled, "but I don't see her being an extrovert all the time as that can be exhausting. Like I said, someone who reads in their spare time, enjoys small town explo-rations, dates at coffee shops and antique stores." He eyed Vivien, who ignored his pointed joke. "Someone who is quietly comfortable wherever she goes and isn't afraid to try new things, either."

Vivien stopped in front of Roman. She perched a hip out and rubbed her chin as she thought.

"You've given me much to think about, Roman, and I'm sure I will find you *exactly* the right woman by Valentine's Day."

"Yeah, okay."

Vivien turned on her heel just as footsteps echoed down the stairway. Roman glanced up at Olivia, just as she landed on the ground floor. She raised a brow at him.

"What are you doing on the floor?"

Roman looked toward Vivien, but she lied motionless on the carpet, just as Sadie had left her. Her lips curled into that coy smile. A chill shivered down Roman's spine.

"I, um, dropped something under the couch. Had to crawl down here to find it."

Olivia stared at him before shaking her head. "Alright, weirdo."

She picked Vivien up off the floor and set her on the coffee table. She asked Roman if he wanted another glass of wine as she stepped into the kitchen.

"No, I'll just have some water," he mumbled as Vivien winked at him.

Chapter Two

Roman woke up the following morning, hungover by his dream of a talking doll. Olivia's husband, Carter, drove him home after the two additional glasses of wine his sister pressured him into — ones that he definitely... totally denied. He dragged himself out of his warm bed and groaned as the sunlight streaming through his window blinded him. He yanked the curtains shut before forcing himself to take a hot shower.

When he came out, he downed the two aspirins that he had left on the nightstand beside his bed. But alongside the small pills, was a playing card. He turned it over in his hand to find the Two of Hearts. He sighed as he set the card down. Now he'd have to go through his decks and find where one card was missing. Great. The things he did while drunk. Roman dressed himself in fresh clothes. The headache wasn't gone, and it threatened to last for most of the day, but he was starting to feel better already.

At the chime of his doorbell downstairs, his gaze faltered. Who could that be on a Saturday afternoon? Surely, not Olivia. He knew she'd be even worse off this morning. Poor Carter had a handful.

Roman tutted down the steep steps of his townhouse before the doorbell chimed again, louder and grating on his ears. He grit his teeth.

"I'm coming!" he called out.

He stopped at the front door and jerked it open with a huff. Only to come face-to-face with a wide doe-eyed blonde. She gasped, her hand perched to ring the bell again. She hurriedly pulled it away.

"Good morning, sir. I'm sorry to have bothered

you so early. But your mail... it was dropped off in my mailbox by accident."

She held out an envelope with his name written neatly across the front. Her long, thin fingers gripped the paper gently. Her nails were painted a soft pink. Her blue eyes peeked out from behind the bouncy blonde curtain of her hair. Roman took the letter, letting his fingers brush against hers. Her cheeks flushed as she looked away.

"Thanks for bringing it over. I appreciate it."

The woman nodded silently, but didn't move to turn away. Roman cleared his throat.

"So, um, are you new to the neighborhood? I've never seen you around here before."

The petite woman nodded slowly. "I just moved in two weeks ago. I live three doors down in 204."

"Ah, well, welcome." Roman smiled gently as anything more might scare the woman away. "I'm, um, I'm Roman."

She chuckled. "I saw... on the letter."

"Oh, right." He scratched the back of his neck.

"I'm Maeve."

"Maeve... is that short for anything?"

She shook her head. "Just Maeve."

Roman smiled, his cheeks aching from the infrequent use of those muscles. "Well, it's very nice to meet you, Just Maeve."

She giggled, her laugh as sweet and as gentle as the rest of her looked.

"Hey, I know we just met and all, but would you like to, um, go get a coffee with me? I have to confess, the place I've been going to is awful and overpriced, and being so new to the area, I don't really know where else to go."

Roman nearly stumbled at her abruptness. Even with all her shy, soft energy, she was forward and unafraid to ask for what she wanted. He liked that.

"Yeah, sure. I'm going to need some caffeine to soothe this hangover anyway. And I know just the place."

"Great! I'll grab my coat and bag, and come back in a minute then."

Maeve scurried back to her door, escaped inside, and within the next twenty minutes, the two of them had planted themselves at a local coffee shop. Maeve ordered a peppermint mocha with extra whipped cream, and Roman had to restrain himself from wiping away the whipped cream mustache on her upper lip. Roman guzzled down his usual cold brew as he watched this woman sigh with pleasure at the first real sip of her hot beverage.

"Oh, Roman. This," she pointed happily at the steaming mug in her hand, "this is what I needed.

Thank you for the recommendation. I never would have found this place on my own."

"I'm just happy to help. And I'm glad you're enjoying the drink." He smiled.

The two of them talked and laughed and joked for hours that day. Roman ordered and bought them gourmet sandwiches for lunch, and Maeve bought them a second round of decaf coffees afterward. Like her appearance, Maeve was warm, soft, easy to make laugh, and easier to make smile. She had many differing interests to Roman, like her love of kayaking and being outdoors — Roman was afraid of open water because of his inability to swim; her love of magazine reading and podcast listening — where Roman preferred to read literature; and her love of traveling and adventuring around the world — when Roman had grown up and stayed in the same small town his entire life.

They were very different people with very different interests. But Maeve... she fit his ideal physical attraction so well. And she was soft, gentle, and sweet. He enjoyed her presence, and he wanted more of it in the future.

He drove them back to the neighborhood that evening and dropped Maeve off at her front door.

"I had a great time today. Thank you for getting me out of the house and humoring me."

Maeve smiled. "Please, it was all my pleasure. Besides, it wasn't completely innocent."

Roman's smile fell. "What do you mean?"

Without warning, Maeve turned him around and pinned him back against her door. Roman's breath caught in his throat, and Maeve's whisper in his ear prickled his skin.

"I've been watching you for two weeks, Roman. You're so delightfully cute and awkward, and I wanted to talk to you much sooner, but I was scared."

Roman whispered. "Why?"

Maeve's smile curled into a crooked grin. She pushed her door open behind him, and Roman stumbled back into the dark. She then closed her door and locked it. And when she flicked the lights on, his eyes widened at what he saw. Pictures of him taped to the wall, scattered across the coffee table, littered on the counter. His breath caught. Maeve stepped forward.

"I've been waiting for this moment, and finally, it's happening." At Roman's wide gaze, she lowered her voice to a gentle whisper, the same tone that had reeled him in that morning. "Don't be afraid, Roman. I'll take good care of you, promise."

The lights flicked out, and Roman lost consciousness as Maeve's footsteps echoed.

He jolted up again in his bed, sweat beaded on his skin, but otherwise, unhurt and safe. The sun shone past his open curtains, and a raging headache rocked his skull. Two aspirins sat on his nightstand, along with a fresh set of clothes — the same set from before — and a playing card. But as he slowly turned the playing card over, expecting the Two of Hearts, he found the Ace of Spades instead.

Chapter Three

Roman locked the door that morning to his bathroom as he showered. He peered over his shoulder as he moved around the house. He flinched at any noise outside, a particularly shrill car horn making his skin crawl and his head pound. He couldn't get the image of Maeve out of his head. Of the pictures of himself plastered on her walls and polluting her home. He thought they had such a good time. She was so sweet, so pleasant, and yet... she had turned out to be a complete psycho.

Should he call the police? But he wasn't hurt, and he *had* woken up in his own bed.

Roman cracked open his laptop and pulled up his work calendar, expecting to see his regular Sunday morning chat-in notes from the closers at his office from the night before. But the calendar was blank. He squinted at the screen. He always had tasks on Sunday morning, so where...?

He glanced at the current date — *Saturday*. What? No, but yesterday—

Roman clicked open his computer calendar, and it also read yesterday's date. He grabbed his phone, and the screen lit up with the same information. Today was... Saturday. Today was yesterday... but how...? Roman glanced at the card on his nightstand. The Ace of Spades sat idly on top of the wood. So dark, so solitary, and not at all the Two of Hearts. He sighed as he grabbed his coat and headed out. He needed some fresh air to clear his head.

As he stepped outside his door, he peered over to unit 204 where Maeve lived, but he paused. There was no petite blonde woman watching him from around the corner. Instead, a moving truck sat in front of the building, and a young family hauled boxes from it into the unit.

Roman watched silently until an older man, maybe the father, stepped outside 204 with empty arms. He caught Roman's eye and waved with a smile. Roman waved back hesitantly before getting into his truck. He sped off down the road, unsure of where he was heading, but he needed to get away. The traffic light ahead of him turned yellow, and he was close enough that he knew he would make it. But as he slid through the intersection just as the light changed to red, another car jumped out. Roman barely had time to gasp before the tire of his truck slammed into the hood of the sedan.

Tires screeched, horns wailed, and Roman's truck skidded forward with the other smaller car in tow. When the screeching vehicles finally came to a halt, Roman gazed wide-eyed and hazily at the damage before him. He blinked once — twice — before he stumbled out of the truck and scrambled to the driver's side of the sedan.

"Hey!" he called out, his voice sounding foreign to his ears, "Hey! Are you okay?"

Roman hunched over and peeked inside the car, but the metal door crashed to the ground and out stepped a dark-haired beauty. A tight leather jacket hugged her wide shoulders, and black skinny jeans accentuated all the right curves. But Roman didn't even have time to appreciate the woman's dark silhouette and glowing brown eyes before her snarl cut him short.

"You hit me!" she shrieked.

Roman had to back up a step. "I... what? No, you hit *me!* I had the right of way through the intersection. The light was still yellow."

The woman rolled her bright eyes. "Which, if you didn't know, means to *slow down*. Not speed up, Einstein."

Roman bristled. "Hey, your front end came flying halfway into the intersection. You pulled up way too fast and way too far."

"If you weren't driving like a maniac and actually paid attention to your surroundings like you're supposed to, we wouldn't even be in this mess." She bit back.

Roman looked at the tall, menacing woman with a biting glare of his own.

"Look, I'm not going to stand here and argue with you. Just give me your insurance information, and I'll call the police. You're going to have to get towed."

The woman turned her vicious glare to the car instead. It softened ever so slightly. "I can't afford to get it towed."

Was this really his problem? He could just call the

police and let them handle the mess. But truthfully, his truck was fine other than some exterior scratches and a dent above his tire. It was her car that was lower to the ground and took the brunt of the damage. It was totaled, most likely. And even if she had pulled into the intersection too soon and too fast, he had also been flying through the light to make it in time.

Roman sighed. "Fine. Look, here is my insurance and contact information. I won't need anything done for my truck, but hopefully, they can work something out for you and your car. And if they need to call me, I can help as needed."

She sighed, taking the scrap of paper from his hand. She stared at it.

"Roman," she murmured.

He nodded. "What's your name?"

She tucked the paper into her pocket. For all her fierce confrontation upfront, she seemed unable to meet his eyes now.

"Hailey."

"Well, I wish we met under better circumstances," he replied lightly.

Hailey looked at him suspiciously. He noted the dark circles under her eyes that matched her dark makeup. All of Roman's fight dissipated.

"Hey, let me call a tow company. I have a buddy who works for them, and he can give us a discount."

Her eyes widened. "Really?"

He nodded. He called his friend, who said he'd be over in ten minutes. Roman hung up, feeling better about the woman and her poor car. He didn't want to contribute to her dark circles. He shivered as a cool gust of winter air blew past them.

"Wanna wait in my truck? The heat still works."

She looked over at his truck with the same suspicion. He chuckled and waved her forward.

"Come on, you'll freeze out here."

Hailey hesitated, but as another brisk wind fluttered through her dark hair, and goosebumps popped up on her face, she jumped into the passenger's seat. Roman turned the heat on full blast, watching Hailey's shivers turn to contented sighs.

"Better?"

She nodded. "The heat in my car doesn't work at all. So, this is... nice."

"It sounds like your car has some issues. More than just a crushed hood." He attempted a light joke, and thankfully, Hailey chuckled.

"Yeah, it's basically a trash heap. But it's all I have right now. It gets me to work and back, and that's what matters."

"What do you do?"

"I'm a mechanic and work primarily on motorcycles. But I also work at a homeless shelter during my free time."

Roman glanced at her. He could see the bike mechanic part from the way she dressed and her hard exterior, but a homeless shelter... that was unexpected.

"What do you do at the homeless shelter?"

"I organize meal times and contact sponsors to get donations for the shelter. Food, clothing, transportation, and experts in the community to come in and teach the people about things that will help them move forward in life."

"Like what?"

"Cooking, cleaning, job applications and interview skills, web applications, computer skills — whatever will help them prosper once they leave the shelter."

Roman stared in awe as Hailey warmed her fingers by one of the vents. This woman, so hard, dark, and fierce — was strong, gentle, and supportive, too. He couldn't look away.

"What do you do?" She glanced up at him, her brown eyes sharp, watchful and warm.

"I'm just another office worker. I work at a publishing company downtown, just doing inventory and data stuff."

"Oh. At Goldfield's?"

"Yeah, you've heard of it?"

"Of course," she said. "I've lived here my entire life."

"You grew up in Alexandra?"

She nodded. "Born and raised. This community has helped raise me, and that's why I want to give back, however I can. Working at the shelter allows me to do that."

"Wow. That's... amazing." Roman smiled. Hailey stared at him and slowly, so slowly — her suspicion shifted into something warmer.

"Have you lived here long?"

"My whole life," Roman stated.

"Do you ever want to leave?"

Roman shook his head. "My whole family is here. My life. I love it here."

Hailey leaned back on the leather seat, the fabric squeaking underneath her weight. She sighed as she watched the moving cars go by.

"All my friends, extended family, dates... they all think I'm crazy for wanting to stay in Alexandra. They tell me that I'm young, with so many opportunities, but let me tell you," she crossed her arms over her chest, "people are nicer in small towns. People care about you and support you when you need help. And Alexandra — this community — has done nothing but help me. Why would I want to leave that?"

Roman smiled. "Exactly."

Hailey turned her gaze to him, and a slow, crooked smile of her own curled her dark lips. Something in Roman's chest fluttered to life. But before he could utter another word, the tow truck pulled up in front of them. Both of them hopped out, braving the cold, as they greeted his friend, Travis. Travis quickly reeled her sedan onto the back of his truck, and Hailey asked him to take it to her workplace. She'd look at it when she could. She asked Travis how much it would cost her for the tow, but he waved her off.

"Nothing for a friend. I'm just glad I could help."

Roman thanked his friend, and Travis nodded with a smile as Hailey looked at him with watery eyes. She thanked him and watched as he turned away, her broken car in tow.

"So, what are your plans now?" Roman asked her.

She shrugged. "I guess my weekend will be spent fixing up my car."

"You think it can be fixed?"

"I just need it to run."

Roman nodded toward his truck. "Hop in then. I'll drive you."

She eagerly jumped back into the warmth of her cab, and he drove them both downtown, following her directions to the shop. Her car sat just outside a garage door, waiting to be taken care of. They both let a long exhale escape their lips as they caught sight of it. They then looked at each other after realizing what they both had done and laughed.

"I'm no good with cars, but can I offer any more help?" he asked.

Hailey raised a brow. "You want to help me?"

"If you'll let me."

Hailey smiled, the motion foreign and tight on her face, but beautiful nonetheless. She waved him after her, and the two of them pushed the broken car into the garage. Hailey assessed the damage while Roman watched. She pulled out a rolling toolbox with tools that Roman didn't recognize, and phrases and parts were called out that he had never heard of as she began working on her car.

Hours went by, and Roman helped as much as he could by handing her tools, offering her drinks when needed, and ordering food for them in the afternoon. This woman wasn't his ideal type in regards to physical features or her career choice, but she was wholesome, funny, energetic, and smart.

Hailey laughed at a poor joke that Roman made as the door opened at the back of the garage. An older man walked in, white hair and angry frown intact. He took one look at Hailey's car, and the frown on his cheeks deepened.

"What the hell did you do?" he yelled.

Hailey rolled her eyes. "I got hit, that's what. And

I'm fine, thanks for asking."

The man tensed, every vein in his arms, every muscle in his neck, pulsing.

"I lent you that car so you could go to and from work, and look at what you've done."

"You *sold* me that trash heap of a car for work, and I used it without complaint, even though *I* had to put too many hours into it just to make sure that it worked in the first place."

"It worked, Hailey. That's all you needed."

"Yes, and it served me well. But it's life appears to have ended." She eyed the shriveled hood. "I got the rest of it working, but the engine won't stick. It's too banged up. And it isn't even worth putting a new one in at this point."

The man glanced over at Roman, perched on his stool.

"Who the hell are you?"

Roman paused. "Um, I'm Roman. Sorry to intrude. I, um, was just trying to help Hailey with her car after our little accide—"

"After I wrecked it this morning," Hailey cut him off. She gave him a pointed look, and Roman tensed as the man did, too.

"So, it was *your* fault. You wrecked the car."

Hailey nodded slowly. "All me. Sorry, Dale."

Dale took a step toward her, and Roman leaned

forward. But Dale was faster. He grabbed Hailey by the hair and yanked her face to within inches of his own. He whispered.

"I gave you this car, this job, this life — you little bitch. And this is how you repay me?"

Roman moved to help, but Hailey gritted her teeth.

"It was an accident. I would never go against you or disrespect your kindness to me on purpose, Dale. You know that."

Dale's lips curled into a snarl, but Hailey looked unfazed. The two stared at each other with cold, hard eyes for a moment longer before he shoved her away. Dale started for the door again.

"Get the engine to work, or you won't have a vehicle. I'll be back tomorrow."

The door slammed shut behind him, and Hailey let out a sigh of relief.

"Who was that?" Roman murmured, moving to her side.

She shook her head with a tight, sad smile on her lips. "Remember when I told you that this town had helped me when I needed it the most, and I wanted to repay the favor?"

Roman nodded.

"Well, Dale was one of the people who gave me a chance and set me on the path forward. He sold me this car for dirt cheap, gave me a job here, and helped get me a cheaper rent for my apartment downtown."

"But he treats you like dirt." Roman noted.

Hailey sat back on her stool and ran a hand through her thick, wavy hair.

"Yeah, well, whether my help was through kindness or threats — my favors have to be repaid. So, here I am."

Roman wanted to say more. He wanted to stick up for her when it seemed like no one else, including Hailey herself, wouldn't. But her somber smile and tired eyes made him pause. They really were two very different people, and he knew next to nothing about her life.

"Hey, you should probably get going. It's getting late, and I have a lot of work left to do here," she said flatly.

"Will you be okay on your own?" Roman eyed the door that Dale had exited through, but she waved him off.

"I'll be fine. Don't worry."

"Okay." Roman pulled out his phone anyway and handed it to her. She looked up at him in confusion. "Your number. I'll text you when I'm home, and I expect you to do the same."

She stared at him, her eyes and open mouth wide in shock. She slowly took his phone, and with shaky fingers, entered her number. He smiled when she handed it back.

"You be safe tonight, and don't stay up too late with this car, okay? If you need help or, more likely, moral support, I'm here."

Her lips cracked into a tight smile, and she nodded.

"Thanks. I appreciate it. Really."

With that, Roman hopped into his own truck outside and made his way back to the townhouse. He texted Hailey after locking the door behind him.

I'm home. :-)

Hailey responded back almost immediately. *Thanks for the company today. I appreciate all your help.*

Roman grinned at his phone before setting it on his nightstand. He watched two episodes of some comedy special on cable, and before he knew it, he nodded off.

When he woke up the next morning, he eagerly grabbed his phone and scrolled through his messages, but nowhere in his history was there a Hailey. He eyed his nightstand in the light of the morning, and on its surface, sat two aspirins, a set of clothes, and a playing card.

Roman's breath hitched as he turned the card over. In the rays of light streaming past his curtains, he came face-to-face with the Queen of Diamonds.

Chapter Four

Roman searched through his contacts, but Hailey's number was nowhere to be seen. He rushed outside after, glanced down at building 204, and found the mailbox decorated with children's handprints and a different last name than he remembered from Maeve's residence. It was like neither of them, Maeve or Hailey, even existed. Had he really met them? Were they real at all? He pulled out his phone and glanced at the screen — *Saturday*, it read.

What was happening? Why was he living Saturday over and over again but differently? Meeting two different women and living two very different days. He must be losing it.

Roman grabbed his coat and moved toward the door, but his phone rang. He paused and stared at the unidentified number on his screen. It had his area code, and while he usually doesn't pick up phone calls from random numbers, something told him to answer this one.

"Hello?" he said, propping the phone to his ear.

A high-pitched woman's voice echoed through the line.

"Hello. Is this Mr. Roman Wright?"

"Yeah. Who's this?"

"Good morning, sir. Sorry to bother you, but we have your niece, Sadie, here at school. She appears to have a slight fever. We contacted her parents but, unfortunately, her father appears to be out of town, and her mother's phone went to voicemail. Your phone number was next in line on the emergency contact list."

"School? Why's she even in school on a Saturday?"

"Don't you know, sir? Sadie comes in with some

other kids on Saturdays for extra tutoring. She's been doing so for months now."

"Oh." Roman threw on his coat, straining his arms through the sleeves as he tried not to drop his phone. "Do you need me to come get her then?"

"Yes, sir. She cannot stay at school with a fever. She needs time and rest to recuperate. I will try to call her mother again, but for now, you will need to come get her."

"Okay. That's fine. I can head out now. I'll be there in five minutes."

"Perfect. We will see you soon."

With that, Roman hung up and raced for his truck. The engine took three or four tries to turn over in the cold morning air, but once it rumbled to life, he floored it out of the parking lot. He made it to Sadie's elementary school in four minutes and rushed to the office. He quickly filled out the necessary paperwork for Sadie's release and then made his way to the nurse's office, where Sadie sat swinging her legs over the side of the nurse's examination bed.

"Uncle Roman!" she called as he smiled at her. He pulled her into a tight hug and stroked her hair.

"Hey, you. Not feeling well?"

She shook her head. "My head was hurting this morning, and Mommy gave me Tylenol, but it didn't work. My head still hurts. So, I came to the nurse, and she took my temperature, and now I have a fever."

"So, she'll need lots of water, rest, and maybe some cool rags for her head." Roman looked up at the honey sweet voice, only to find a red-headed woman perched in the doorway to the desk area of the school infirmary. She smiled at him before meeting Sadie's eyes. "Get some Gatorade on your way home, alright? The electrolytes will help. Once you're home, it's straight to bed and lots of rest, okay?"

Sadie nodded sharply. "Yes, Ms. Miller."

Ms. Miller smiled. "Good. Now, Mr. Wright, if you'll step into my office for a moment, I just need you to sign a few papers, and you two can be on your way."

Roman nodded and followed the woman into her office space. She closed the door behind her and pulled out the extra chair beside her desk.

"Have a seat." Once he sat down, she set three sheets of paper in front of him. "I need you to read and sign the bottom of each one. The first goes over the patient release information and acceptance; that one's for the school's records. The next is for the state, acknowledging that I examined and treated Sadie to the best of my abilities as her nurse. And the final one is for my records, just acknowledging Sadie's visit, her complaints, symptoms, and the resolution. Which, obviously, was to send her home with you."

"Okay." Roman signed each one after skimming their contents. Once he finished, she stacked the papers into a neat pile and set them on the center of her desk.

"Wonderful! Thank you for coming to get Sadie today. I tried her mom again, but she didn't answer. I hope she's alright."

"It *is* odd. I'll try her after I get Sadie home. But thank you for taking care of her, Ms. Miller."

"Oh, you can call me Brielle." She smiled easily. Her painted pink lips were peachy and smooth against her freckled skin and burning red hair.

"Well, thank you again, Brielle." Roman smiled, too.

They both moved for the door, but before Roman could push it open, it was yanked away from him from the opposite side. A sweaty and panting Olivia stood in the doorway.

"Sadie, is she okay?" She gasped before noticing Roman. "Romy? What are you doing here?"

"The nurse called me when she couldn't get a hold of you. I came to get Sadie."

Brielle stepped out from behind him and waved at Olivia.

"Hello, Mrs. Finkle. I apologize for the confusion and anxiety. Sadie is doing just fine. She just has a slight fever and needs to rest at home."

"Oh." Olivia turned as Sadie ran up to her side and gripped her forearm with a smile.

"Mommy, I'm ready to go home now."

Olivia glanced at the three of them and nodded slowly as the panic seemed to slip away. She patted Sadie's head. "Okay, sweetie. We're going." She waved at the two of them before grabbing Sadie's backpack and turning out of the infirmary.

Roman let out a short sigh. "Well, I guess she's got her then."

Brielle chuckled lightly. "You're off the hook."

"Guess so." He scratched the back of his neck.

"Do you have any children of your own here?"

"No," he said, "just Sadie, my niece."

"And yet, you came so quickly."

"Yeah. I mean, Sadie was sick and needed help. Why wouldn't I come quickly?"

Brielle chuckled as she settled back into the chair behind her desk. "You'd be surprised how many parents take their good ol' time when I call them, telling them their children are sick and need to be picked up. So, the fact that Sadie isn't even yours, and you still came very quickly — you must really care about her."

Roman nodded easily. "She's my niece, my only niece. She means the world to me, and I'd do anything for that kid."

Brielle smiled up at him. "That's good to know. I mean, if she ever falls ill again, and I can't contact her parents, of course."

"Of course." Roman chuckled.

"Hey, I know this may seem a bit out there and probably, totally, unprofessional, but are you free tonight?"

Roman paused in the doorway. Had he heard her right?

"You... you're asking me out?"

Brielle smirked, her white nurse's coat hanging around her shoulders and draping past the hemline of her skirt so perfectly that it looked like there might just be nothing underneath the white lab coat. Until she shifted, of course. She crossed her thick thighs and caused the skirt to rise a little higher on her skin as she turned to him.

"I probably shouldn't be, but yes, I am. I'm, um, going to a party with some friends at the bar tonight, and no matter how many times I've told them that I don't need a man at my side or a boyfriend, they pester me nonstop about my lack of a date. And while I was mentally preparing all morning to listen to those teasing remarks all night, you stepped in. Young, handsome, and caring. And honestly, what else could I ask for?"

Roman was speechless. This woman — curvy and

beautiful and smart and sweet — wanted to go out with him. After only knowing him for twenty minutes. After only talking to him once. All because he loved Sadie and was worried for her health.

Roman glanced at the clock on the far wall. It was still early afternoon, and being that it was Saturday, yet again, he had nothing else to do. He shrugged.

"Why not? I'll be your date."

Brielle nearly squealed with delight. "Really? Wait, seriously?"

"Yeah." Roman chuckled nervously. "You *were* being serious, right?"

"Yes! Oh, yes. Completely! I just didn't think — oh! This is perfect! Thank you, Roman, or is it Romy?"

"Roman is just fine."

"Classy and original. I adore it." She actually squealed this time as she walked him to the door. "Okay, I will send you a message with the time and everything, and meet you there. Dress casual; it's just a bar, you know? Oh, thank you, thank you, Roman! I really appreciate it. Really, you can't even imagine the amount of pestering you've saved me from."

Roman chuckled. "It's no problem. I'll see you tonight."

"Yes! See you tonight!" Brielle turned on her heel

back into the office, and Roman grinned as he heard her squeal in her office.

He made his way down the hall and out to his truck. His phone beeped as he started the engine. He glanced at it and found a text from a new number. It said they were meeting tonight at eight and thanked him *again* for coming. It was signed "Bri."

Roman smiled to himself as he drove home. He spent the rest of the afternoon cleaning his house, and then himself before the evening. By the time eight rolled around, he sat outside the bar in his truck, his hair damp from the shower and styled just perfectly messy, his jawline covered with a light shadow, and his body dressed in a button-down shirt with his favorite jeans that fit just right. But as he stepped inside the bar and glanced around for Brielle, he didn't find a buttoned-up nurse in a lab coat. Instead, a woman found his eyes from across the room. She smiled, the only thing similar to the woman he had spoken to that morning. The rest of her, however, made his jaw drop.

She wore a tight skirt that came up to her mid-thigh, with thigh-high socks that stretched up and squeezed, revealing that tiniest hint of skin on her legs. High boots hugged her calves and accentuated her long legs. And a sparkly belt around her pink lace top cinched her waist into a perfect hourglass shape. Her pink lips had shifted into a dark, almost blood red, shade, making her green eyes shimmer and her freckled skin glow. Her hair burned like fire under the rotating bar lights. They shifted red as she made her way over to him, and he saw nothing but a fierce being of fire and flame.

"Hey, I'm glad you made it," she called out once she was close enough for him to hear over the music and loud chatter.

Roman followed her to her group. "Wouldn't miss it. Like Sadie, I didn't want to leave you stranded."

She chuckled. "I appreciate that." She stopped at the edge of a round table surrounded by five other people. Three females and two males. They all looked at him with either skepticism or wonder. He swallowed down his uneasiness and forced a smile instead.

"This is Roman, my *date*," Brielle emphasized.

The girls' eyes widened with excitement while the guys looked at him.

"This is him? Wow, good choice, Bri. He *is* cute."

"Totally. Where'd you snatch him?" Two of the girls chimed.

Brielle smiled at him. "At work. He came to pick up his niece. He was so good with her; I couldn't take my eyes off him."

Roman nodded a little too quickly.

"Aw," one girl cooed, "a *daddy*."

Brielle gave her friend a light shove, and they all

giggled. Roman wavered. He wasn't used to this social life — late nights at a bar, outings with big groups of friends, introductions, first impressions...

Roman always stayed within his circle. His tight little circle of family and friends. He enjoyed spending time with them regularly and attending the occasional party, but this? This was way out of his comfort zone. What was he even doing here? Why did he say yes? The lights spun too fast and too bright, the music beat too loudly, thumping through his limbs and vibrating his bones; the people surrounding him all reeked of pungent cologne and sweat, and this place was unapologetically stuffy. He preferred the cold February air outside over this.

Brielle laughed at something that one of her male friends had said. At her smile, Roman's panic curbed the slightest bit. He was there to support her. He told her he would, and he wouldn't back out now just because he felt outside his comfort zone.

"She's a beauty, isn't she?" A female voice echoed to his left. He glanced up and found a pair of brown eyes on him. She was one of Brielle's friends.

Roman followed her gaze to Brielle. He smiled. "She is. Her laugh, her charm, her ease... it's contagious."

Her friend nodded, her smile warming. "Do you like her? I know she said you're her date for tonight, but we all figured she begged you to come last minute to avoid our teasing."

"You knew," he mumbled, but his smile only widened as Brielle looked up to lock eyes with him. Her red lips curled into a wide grin, and something in his chest tightened. "She's the complete opposite of me, but she's... well... I do like her."

Her friend made room as Brielle climbed onto the bench beside him. They all spent the night talking, laughing, gossiping about small town life. Roman admittedly felt anxious at first, but as the night came to a close, and Brielle gave him a peck on the cheek before driving off with her friends, he couldn't help but feel happy.

Chapter Five

Roman woke up the following morning expecting sunshine through his window, the curtain pushed aside, and a headache behind his eyes. But when he opened his eyes, it was raining outside his window. He sat up and tilted his head, but the headache had disappeared, too.

He glanced down at his nightstand, expecting two

aspirins, his clothes, and the standard playing card of the day. But none of those were there. His table sat empty except for his phone. He picked it up, and the screen flickered to life.

Sunday.

Something white sat on the nightstand underneath where his phone was. His eyes turned on it and found another playing card. He picked it up and turned it over slowly. It was the Joker.

A crash from the kitchen steeled his spine. Roman grabbed the bat that he kept in his closet and crept down the stairs. Each step creaked under his weight, and he flinched at the noise. But the crashes in the kitchen didn't stop. He rounded the last corner to the room and paused as he peeked in, and there, on the kitchen island, sat Vivien the doll on the napkin holder. She sipped from a tiny teacup, unbothered by his ensuing presence.

"What? How? What are you doing here?" He gaped as he threw down the bat.

She barely glanced up at him. "Good to see you again, Roman."

"Vivien... what?"

"I'm here for your decision, Roman."

"What are you talking about?"

"Don't play dumb. Surely, you've noticed the last

three Saturdays you've gotten to enjoy with three very different women."

Roman thought back to the cards, the date on his phone, the identical setting each morning…

Vivien pulled three cards from the tabletop. She held them up one by one.

"The Two of Hearts. Sweet, quiet, and warm. Cute, right? Maeve fits your desired physical traits to the dot. But that obsessive personality, it's… interesting.

"The Ace of Spades. Dark, mysterious, independent. Hailey is a fiery one, and so wholesome, too. But the baggage she carries…" Vivien blew out a low whistle.

"And the Queen of Diamonds. Wild, strong, and hot. Brielle was almost the opposite of what you described in a woman, but she's also a nurse and loves children. She'd probably push you out of your comfort zone."

"They were all great, at first. Each of them had traits that I liked," Roman answered slowly.

Vivien nodded. "But…?"

"But they were also so different from my ideal. And so different from me. Maeve seemed perfect in all regards, but she turned out to be a bit… psychotic. Hailey *is* wholesome but carries too much on her shoulders. And Brielle loves kids and helps them like I wanted, but her social life is way out of my comfort zone."

"I see." Vivien looked at him, that coy grin still on her lips. "So, none of the women suited your ideal just right."

Roman wavered. He enjoyed his time with all the women and had come to like them. But he saw the issues that would emerge in the future if he were to pursue them. Maeve's obsession was a no-brainer, Hailey's baggage would catch up to her and maybe drag her down forever, and Brielle was too extroverted; she'd grow bored of Roman and look elsewhere for fulfillment.

"I just don't see any of the relationships working long-term."

"So, you choose none?"

Roman eyed the cards on the table and thought back on the last three days. But all he could see was the obsessiveness, the baggage, and the extroversion; none of these women were just right for him.

"I choose none... for now."

Vivien's smile cracked into a wide grin. "That's unfortunate. And I thought Hailey and Brielle had a solid chance. Oh, well."

"They were great. But the differences between us were too significant. Would you be able to summon another woman?"

Vivien pulled the last card from the tabletop and held it up to him. The Joker.

"No, Roman, I can't. Because this is the end of the line for you."

"What do you mean? I thought you were going to get me a perfect woman before Valentine's Day."

"I did. Three of them, in fact. Three of them who suited your needs in some way. But like any living person on this Earth, they didn't fit your ideal to the very last dot. Because human beings are all unique, all of them have strengths and weaknesses, and things that set them apart from everyone else. And you, Roman, *still* chose none of them."

"Wait, but I—"

"There's a deal with my game here. I give you three women, and you choose which one you'd like to keep in your lonely little life. If you choose, *boom*! She's yours. But if you see only the negatives, only the traits that the women *don't* have, and choose none of them, well," she tilted her porcelain little head at him, "then you get nothing."

"But you... but—"

Vivien slinked off the napkin holder and dropped the Joker onto the table, right on top of the other cards.

"Even when three amazing women were dropped

at your feet, you still chose none of them." She shook her head. "You deserve to rot alone, Roman."

"Wait, Vivien, I—"

"Oh, well, off to my next adventure. Enjoy your pitiful, lonely life, Roman."

Before he could say another word to stop her, she vanished. Roman stared at the spot where she had been, the four cards staring up at him, accusing him, taunting him for his mistake. He left them there until the following Saturday, and then he threw them into the trash. For this Valentine's Day and all the ones following, he spent alone.

The End

About the Author

Viola Tempest is a dystopian fantasy and paranormal romance author who yearns to expose the truth of those in the modern world: the good, the bad, and the ugly. Her inspiration primarily stems from life experiences, those who annoy her, ex-boyfriends, and the crazy dreams that pop into her head every once in a while.

Stalk her below!

* * *

Website:

https://www.violatempest.com/

Facebook Page:

https://www.facebook.com/authorviolatempest

Instagram:

https://www.instagram.com/author_violatempest/

Goodreads:

https://www.goodreads.com/author/show/21693342.
Viola_Tempest

Bookbub:

https://www.bookbub.com/authors/viola-tempest

Game of HEARTS

ENCHANTED WISHES COLLECTION

VIOLA TEMPEST